The Lion
and the Mouse

Once upon a time, in a jungle far, far away, lived a mighty lion named Jato. He was the King of the Jungle, ruler of all the creatures that lived there. The jungle animals loved their king, but were always a bit nervous around him because he had a ferocious set of teeth!

One day, after he'd finished his breakfast, Jato wondered what to do. He soon decided that today, like most days, was a great day to visit some of his royal subjects and explore his kingdom.

"I think I'll go see the monkeys this morning," Jato said to himself. "They are a chatty bunch, and always have a new joke to tell me. After that, maybe I'll go for a swim."

With that, Jato set off toward the grove where the monkeys lived.

At the monkeys' tree, Jato announced himself with a roar.

"Quit monkeying around!" he said. "The King of the Jungle is here."

Old Mort, the leader of the monkeys, bowed to Jato. The other monkeys chattered to each other, excited to see their king.

"How may I be of service, Your Majesty?" asked Mort.

"I've come to hear a joke," Jato replied.

Mort grinned a big monkey grin. He had a great new joke to share, and was sure that the king would like it!

"What time is it when an elephant sits on your house?"
Mort asked.

"What time..." Jato repeated. He was stumped!

"Why, it's time to get a new house!" Mort said.

Jato roared with laughter. What a funny joke!

"That was an excellent joke, Mort." Jato said. "I'll come see you again soon. But now, I am going swimming."

"Be careful, King Jato," Mort warned. "My scouts spotted some strange creatures near the river yesterday."

Jato was surprised to hear this. He wondered who the strange creatures were, and decided to find out for himself.

As Jato walked deeper into the jungle, he said hello to the warthogs, parrots, cheetahs, and all of the other animals he saw. He asked each one about the strange creatures by the river, but no one else had seen or heard them.

When Jato reached the river, he didn't see anything unusual. He jumped into the cool water and paddled around. He had so much fun that he soon forgot all about the strange creatures. After a while, Jato laid down for a nap. All that swimming had tired him out!

Meanwhile, a little mouse named Mazy scurried toward the river. He was busily searching for berries and nuts to feast on, and didn't notice the sleeping lion.

Mazy climbed over a rock, walked along a fallen log, and then hopped onto Jato. He scurried up the lion's back, through his thick mane, and down the lion's nose. There were no nuts or berries there, that's for sure!

Mazy was just about to jump off the tip of the lion's nose when Jato's big paw reached up and grabbed him.

Mazy yelped in surprise. He hadn't realized that he'd crawled onto a lion... but this wasn't just any lion, it was King Jato! Jato held Mazy in his giant paws and blew hot air into his face.

"Who dares to disturb the King of the Jungle?" Jato growled.

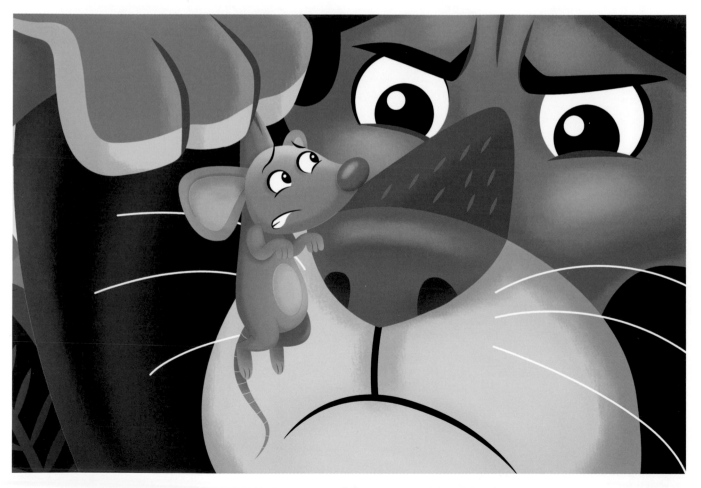

"M-m-my name is Mazy," the little mouse stammered as he stared at Jato's sharp teeth. "I didn't mean to disturb you!"

"Just what do you think you're doing, waking me from my nap?" asked Jato. "I'm so mad, I could eat you!"

"Pardon me, Your Majesty," Mazy squeaked. "I really didn't mean to wake you. Please don't eat me!"

Jato had eaten a big breakfast and wasn't really hungry. But he knew that he must be stern with the jungle creatures, and tightened his grip on the mouse. He growled, and poor Mazy trembled with fright.

"Tell me, Mazy, why I shouldn't eat you," Jato said.

"If you let me go," Mazy said, gathering his courage, "I will remember your kindness. One day, when you need help, I'll return the favor."

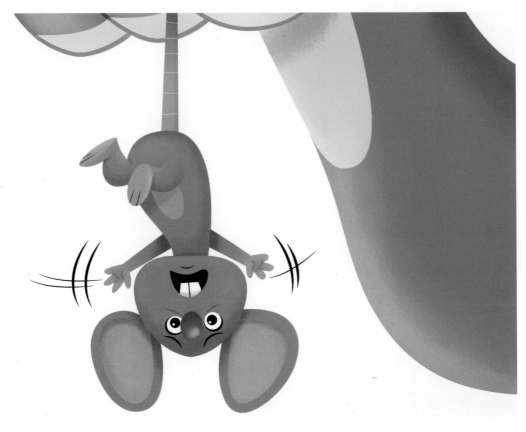

"Now, just how could a teeny mouse help a big, strong lion like me?" Jato asked.

"Everyone needs help some time or another," Mazy replied. "Maybe I'll save your life one day."

Jato was impressed with the mouse's bravery. It takes a lot of courage to stand up for yourself, especially when you're talking to the King of the Jungle!

"You're free to go," Jato said. "I hope you learned your lesson about waking me!"

"Yes, Your Majesty, of course!" Mazy replied. "And don't forget my promise to help you. Just let me know when you need me."

With that, Mazy ran away as fast as his little legs would carry him.

A few days later, Jato heard the monkey troop screeching. They were swinging through the trees in quite a hurry.

"King Jato!" Mort yelled. "The strange creatures returned to the river last night! We think they were humans."

Humans had never come so deep into the jungle before. All of the jungle animals knew that humans were dangerous. They could even hurt a lion if they wanted to! Jato decided to go to the river to investigate.

When he neared the river, Jato moved slowly and quietly.
If the humans were there, he didn't want them to hear him coming.
He stopped behind a big bush and peered from side to side. He didn't
see anyone unusual, or hear any unfamiliar voices.

Jato was almost at the edge of the river when he got tangled up in something. He fell to the ground with a startled growl. He tried to stand up, but he couldn't move his legs. He was caught in a net! But who would lay a net on the jungle floor?

Jato suddenly realized that the strange creatures the monkeys had seen were not just humans... they were hunters!

Jato tried to free himself, but he just couldn't claw his way out. He knew that he had to hurry. His life was in danger! He had to get free before the hunters returned. He roared angrily.

Across the jungle, Mazy was snacking on a nut. When he heard a loud roar echoing through the trees, he knew that it was Jato. He sounded like he was in trouble!

"King Jato needs me!" Mazy cried as he dropped the nut. "I'm coming, Your Highness!"

When he reached the riverbank, Mazy was shocked to see the King of the Jungle caught in a net. He rushed over to help.

"Have no fear, Mazy is here!" he cried.

"Oh, Mazy!" Jato said. "You've got to get me out of here!"

Mazy quickly set to work. He chewed through one vine, and then another, and another.

Soon enough, the mouse had made a hole that was big enough for Jato to crawl out of. The big lion shook himself. It felt good to be free!

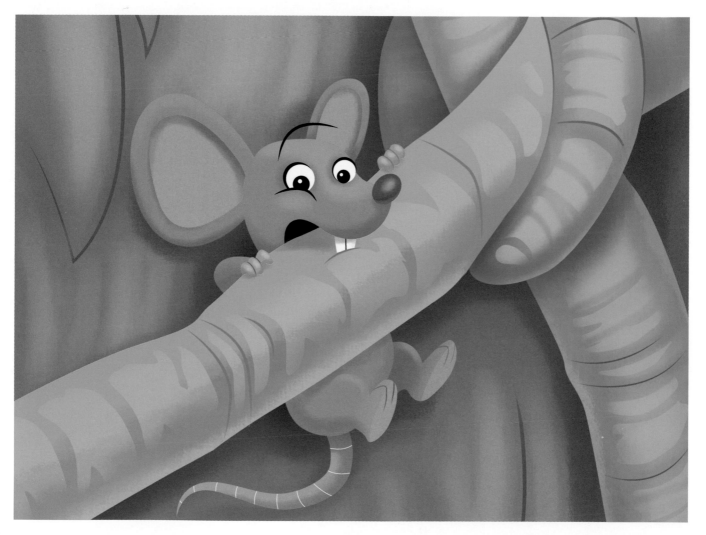

Mazy had saved King Jato! He was very proud of himself.

"Thank you, Mazy," Jato said. "You saved my life! And you taught me an important lesson: even the smallest creature can do great things."

From that day on, Jato and Mazy were the best of friends. The hunters were never spotted again, and King Jato continued to happily rule the jungle for many, many years.